Jim and Slim's Lighthouse Adventure

Written by June Jennings

Illustrated by Sophie Holme

Printed by Badger Press, Bowness

There once was a pirate and he was called Jim,
And he had a mate and he was called Slim.
They'd heard a tale from their good friend Mouse,
Of a ship that had sunk by an old lighthouse.

So they set sail
to look for the wreck,
Hoping to find
some treasure on its deck.

But it started to thunder
and it started to hail,
And soon those pirates
were caught in a gale.

Then just when they thought
that the mast might go,

They heard a loud

Yo ho ho

"Do you need a hand?" came a voice they knew,
It was Pirate Pearl and her mate Soo.

"Great", called Jim, "could you tow us along?"
"Sure", shouted Pearl, and then Soo sang a song . . .

"Yo ho ho, if you sail our seas,
You'd better watch out for we do
what we please.
You can pay us with gold or whatever
you've got,
Jewels or silver, we don't mind what!"

Jim paid Pearl well as
their ships drew near,
Soo said to Slim,
"what brings you round here?"
So he told her about their good friend Mouse,
And that they were looking for
an old lighthouse.

Don't tell them about the wreck!

Then they waved goodbye . . .
but with gold on her mind,
Pearl thought she'd follow to
see what they'd find.

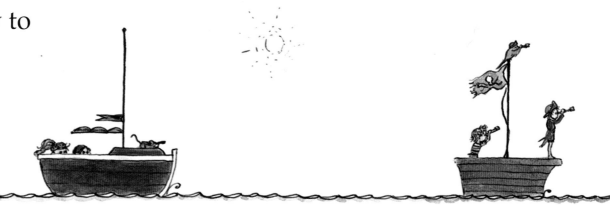

So they followed all day . . .

and they followed all night . . .

Hmm . . .
I bet they're
after treasure!

then they heard
someone yell . . .

They sailed to the lighthouse, Slim tied to a pier,
"Come on", called Jim, "the wreck must be near".

They jumped in the water, with torches in hand . . .

. . . And discovered the ship,
half-buried in sand.

There on the deck were barrels galore . . .

So they cut one loose and dragged it ashore.

But then those two pirates got quite a shock,
     When some strangers jumped out from behind a huge rock.
They looked really mean and one of them said,
     "This island is ours and I'm Captain Ned!"

Nobody spoke, but they all went to look,
As Ned opened the barrel with his rusty old hook.
But what a surprise when they saw what was there,
Big jars of honey that belonged to a . . .

. . . Bear!

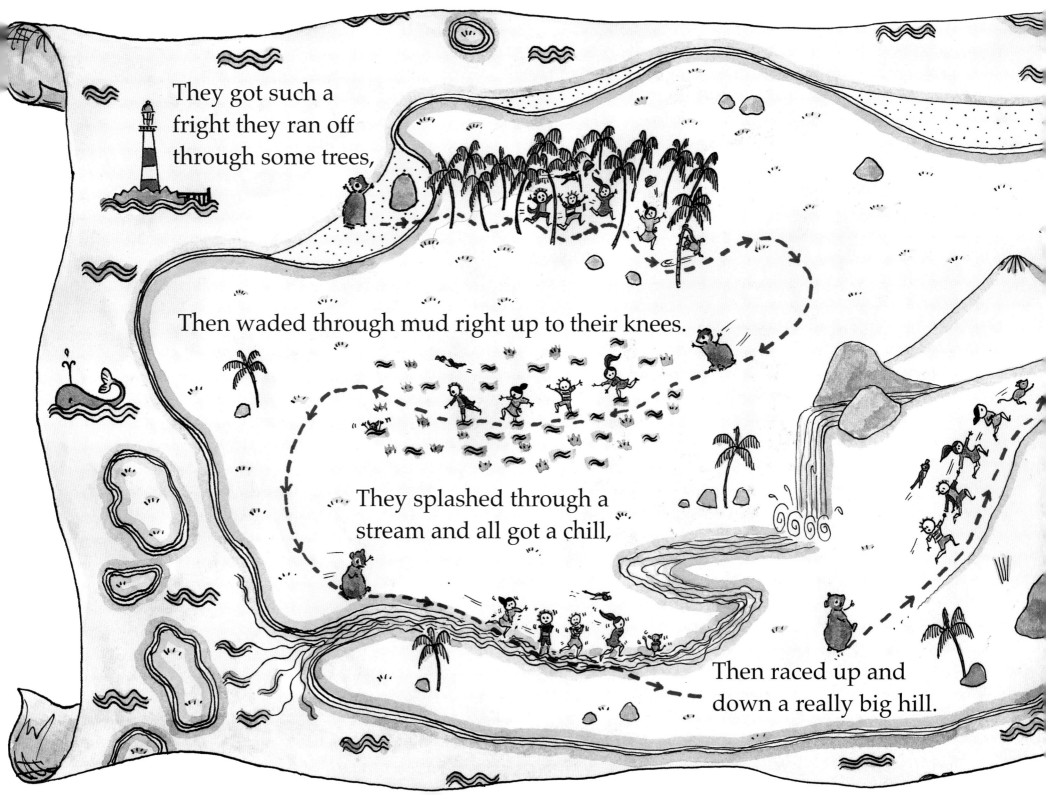

They got such a fright they ran off through some trees,

Then waded through mud right up to their knees.

They splashed through a stream and all got a chill,

Then raced up and down a really big hill.

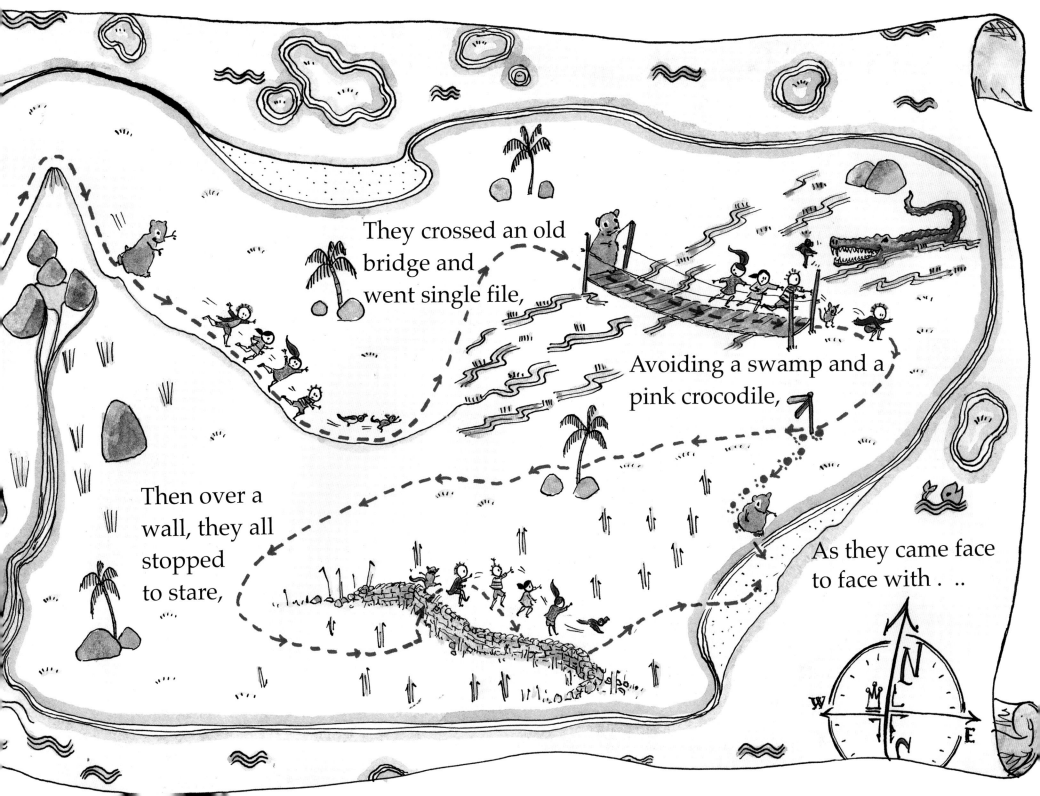

They crossed an old bridge and went single file,

Avoiding a swamp and a pink crocodile,

Then over a wall, they all stopped to stare,

As they came face to face with . . .

. . . that same hairy bear!

"Don't worry", said Bear, "it's really alright,

I'm not going to eat you and I don't even bite".

Then looking around at the raggedy bunch,

Said, "you all look quite tired, so how about lunch?"

Pearl and Soo said, "sorry you lot,
   Hope you're not mad at our little plot!"
Then they laughed and chatted with Bear all day long,
   Slim told some jokes and Soo sang a song.

Then Bear told them how he had lost his way,
And crashed his ship in Lighthouse Bay.

Jim said, "Bear, you've had some bad luck,
    And without your ship, you're really quite stuck.
If we could just get all those barrels to float,
    I think we could build you a really good boat".

And guess what?

. . . It really was a good boat,
and Bear loved it!

Slim's Jokes

Q. Why do pirates have hooks?

A. Because their coats would fall on the floor without them!

Q. What kind of a house can you pick up?

A. A lighthouse!

Q. When did the bear learn to tie knots?

A. When he was a cub!

Q. Why are pirates good at sailing?

A. Because they just Arrrrr!

Q. Why couldn't the pirates play cards?

A. Because they were standing on the deck!

Q. Why did the parrot stand on the fish?

A. Because it was a perch!